Okomi had seen Mama Du climb up trees to pick leaves. He was feeling adventurous and today he wanted to try.

Okomi had only climbed small trees before, but this was a very tall tree. Bravely, Okomi began to inch his way up.

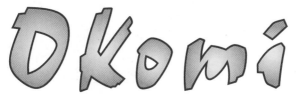

Okomi
climbs a tree

Helen and Clive Dorman
Illustrated by Tony Hutchings

Produced by The Children's Project in association with

Roots & Shoots

THE
JANE GOODALL
INSTITUTE-UK

CP Publishing

It was early morning. Okomi and his mummy, Mama Du, were on one of their walks.

It had rained heavily during the night and all around them leaves glistened with drops of water.

Okomi spotted a branch with some tasty new leaves, high up in a tree.

The wet tree trunk gleamed in the sunshine. It was very, very slippery.

Oh! Careful Okomi, you nearly slipped.

The branch was just within his reach, but as he made a grab for it, he missed, and began to slip...

Poor Okomi slid down towards the ground clutching the trunk as tightly as he could.

Down he went, faster and faster...

Thud!

Okomi had landed on some soft leaves so he was not hurt.

'Hoo, Hoo, Hoo!' He whimpered.

Mama Du looked round. She was used to Okomi's bumps, so she carried on foraging for food.

Okomi sat very still for a while looking at the wet tree trunk in front of him.

Okomi sat up, shook himself and gazed up at the branch.
He got up and once again tried to climb the tree.

First, he put one arm around the tree trunk, then one leg. Then the other arm, and then the other leg. Using all his strength he climbed up the tree.

Up and up he went.

The leaves got nearer and nearer.

Okomi reached out to the branch and this time – he made it.

Well done Okomi!

Okomi sat on the branch. At last he could pick and eat the precious tasty green leaves.

When Okomi had finished his meal he wanted to get down.

But how could he get down?
Oh no, he was stuck!

Okomi was frightened and whimpered loudly in distress.

Mama Du had been keeping an eye on Okomi, so she was not surprised when he started whimpering.

Mama Du climbed the tree.

She tried to lift Okomi off the branch but he was clinging on too tightly.

Poor Okomi was getting more and more frightened and tired.

Mama Du kept gently persuading Okomi to let go. After a few attempts he did!

He sprung into his mummy's arms, safe at last. He grunted softly as she cuddled him.

Mama Du had rescued him!

By now, the sun had dried the tree trunk. Okomi felt brave again and climbed down all by himself.

Well done Okomi, you did it!

> "Every individual matters.
> Every individual has a role to play.
> Every individual makes a difference."
> *Jane Goodall*

Michael Neugebauer

Did you know?

Chimpanzees love to hug and kiss their friends and family. There are close bonds between family members. They are very intelligent.

When they are very young, baby chimpanzees cling to their mother's tummy.

When they are about six months old, baby chimpanzees start to ride on their mother's back.

At about the same age they start learning to walk and to climb trees.

Young chimps remain with their mothers until they are seven or eight years old.

Chimpanzees in the wild can live for as long as 50 years.